Dolphin School

Pearl's Ocean Magic

Dolphin School

Pearl's Ocean Magic

by Catherine Hapka
illustrated by Hollie Hibbert

SCHOLASTIC INC.

For Becky Shapiro,
who started the magic

ISBN 978-0-545-75024-0

15 14 13   21 22/0

Printed in the U.S.A.   40
First printing, January 2015
Book design by Jennifer Rinaldi Windau

1

First Day of School

"Do you think the other dolphins at school will like me?" Pearl asked.

She was swimming through the blue waters of the Salty Sea with her pod. A pod is a dolphin family. Pearl's pod was made up of herself, her parents, and her little sister, Squeak.

"Of course they'll like you!" Pearl's father told her.

Pearl's mother slowed down to let a school

of fish swim by. The sun made the silvery little fish sparkle in the clear water. The sea was shallow here among the beautiful coral reefs that grew all over the area.

"Just be yourself, Pearl," Pearl's mother said. "You'll make lots of friends."

Pearl hoped her parents were right. Her pod was much smaller than most and lived in a quiet lagoon far away from other pods.

That meant Pearl hardly ever saw other young dolphins. Well, except for Squeak, of course. But she was too young to count.

"I'm sure you'll love school, Pearl," her father said. "You want to learn how to use your magic, right?"

"That's true." Pearl blew a stream of bubbles out of her blowhole as she thought about that. Dolphins were the protectors of the ocean. They helped other sea creatures whenever they could. The reason Pearl and her pod lived in their lagoon was because sea turtles laid their eggs on the beach nearby. Pearl's pod helped the baby turtles swim safely out to sea after they hatched.

Most of the time that was an easy job. All the dolphins had to do was steer the tiny creatures into deeper waters or show them where to find food. Pearl's parents used a special magical skill called *guiding* to do that. It made the turtles want to do whatever the dolphins were thinking. Magical guiding could also help the hatchlings swim faster to escape from hungry crabs and fish.

But that wasn't the only type of dolphin magic Pearl's parents used. For instance, the dolphins could sing magical songs, or create sparkly light displays in the water to distract the gulls that liked to swoop down and snatch the baby turtles out of the shallows.

Pearl wanted to be able to do all of those things someday, just like her parents. She was already good at using mental magic to communicate with the baby turtles and other sea creatures. Dolphins were the only ones who could send mental messages to one another using words and ideas, though all fish and animals understood the simple pictures and emotions that the dolphins sent. Pearl and Squeak practiced that kind of mental magic all the time. They could use their skills to talk an octopus into playing with them, or to convince a pair of cranky crabs to stop fighting. The dolphin sisters were pretty good at sending more complicated messages to each other, too, even when they were half a lagoon apart. And now, finally, Pearl was old enough to go to school and learn the rest of her dolphin skills.

"I can't wait until I'm old enough to go to school!" Squeak flapped her fins. "What classes will you take, Pearlie?"

"Magic class, of course," Pearl told her sister. "I can't wait to start that one! I'll also be taking Music, Ocean Lore, and Jumping and Swimming."

"I'm going to be great at Jumping and Swimming!" Squeak demonstrated by zipping to the surface and leaping into the air. Then she swam back down, dodging around a prickly bit of fire coral. "Wait, but what's Ocean Lore?" she asked.

"That's where you'll learn all about our world here in the Salty Sea," Pearl's father explained, wiggling his flukes—his tail fins— to move forward. "You'll also learn more about the other creatures who live here with us, like fish and lobsters and jellyfish and—"

"Oh!" Pearl's mother broke in suddenly. "Someone is in trouble!"

Pearl had seen it, too. An image had just popped into her mind. It was shadowy and dark and filled with fear.

"Here!" Pearl's father led the way past another coral formation.

A spotted eel was thrashing around near the reef. His long, slender body was all tangled up in something white and crinkly. He shook and jerked his whole body trying to get loose from it. He was so frantic that he kept slamming into the spiky coral.

"Stop!" Pearl's father cried. "Hold still, friend. We want to help you."

Pearl could feel magic energy flowing out toward the eel from both her parents. But the eel only thrashed harder.

"He's panicking," Pearl's father said. "He doesn't even hear us."

"Come," Pearl's mother told her children. "Join in. We need to get through to him before he hurts himself."

Pearl and Squeak swam forward. Pearl focused her mind on the eel and sent a mental message. *Peace, friend*, she thought. *Be still so we can help you.*

She knew the eel wouldn't understand the words of her message. But she hoped he would feel that the dolphins were trying to help.

"It's still not working," Pearl's father said after a moment.

Pearl's mother swam forward, letting the eel's body slam against her sleek gray side instead of the sharp coral. Once again, Pearl felt strong magic flowing out from her mother.

"Is she guiding the eel?" Squeak whispered.

"I think so," Pearl replied. "She might even be pushing him."

Pushing was a stronger form of magical

guiding. Usually dolphins tried not to use it, since it forced other creatures to do what the dolphins wanted rather than allowing them a choice. But sometimes, in an emergency, pushing was necessary. Pearl kept focusing on the eel, adding her tiny bit of magic to the stronger magic coming from her parents.

This time, it worked. The eel's frantic motions slowed, and then stopped. He hung in the water, still and dull-eyed.

"Hurry," Pearl's mother said. "I can't push him to stay still for long. Get him untangled."

Pearl zipped forward to help her father and sister. They pulled at the white substance with their snouts.

"Yuck," Squeak said, spitting out a piece that had come loose in her mouth. "What is this junk, anyway?"

"It must be something the Land Leggers dropped in the water," her father replied.

Land Leggers were a species of two-legged creature that lived on the islands and shore above the surface of the Salty Sea. Pearl had never seen one, since there were none on the turtles' island. But she'd seen lots of things that had washed into the sea from the Land Leggers' world.

"There—I think the eel is loose," her father said. "Back away in case he panics when your mother releases him."

Pearl and her family backed off. Her mother stopped her flow of magic energy. The eel hung there in the water for a moment. Then, with a single flip of his whiplike body, he disappeared into a hole in the coral. A grateful feeling floated into Pearl's mind, and she smiled in the direction of the eel.

"How far are we from dolphin school?" Squeak wondered.

Her father nodded his sleek gray head toward a coral wall nearby. "We're here."

Pearl realized he was right. Coral Cove Dolphin School was located in a shallow lagoon protected by a colorful ring of coral reef.

"Thanks for swimming me to school," she told her parents and sister when they reached the entrance.

"You're welcome," her mother said. "Will you be okay swimming home by yourself after school?"

"I think so." Pearl wiggled her fins nervously.

"Just remember to stay away from Bigsky Basin," Pearl's father said. "The water is very deep there."

"Yeah," Squeak said. "There could be sharks!"

Pearl shivered as she glanced up at her father's dorsal fin. There was a scar there. Long ago, a shark had bitten him while his pod was rescuing an octopus from becoming the shark's dinner. Pearl had heard the story many times. But it seemed even scarier here, so close to Bigsky Basin.

"Maybe your new school friends will swim you home," Squeak told Pearl.

"Maybe." Pearl forgot about sharks as she looked into the school lagoon. Inside, she could see lots of dolphins of all ages swimming around. "But what if nobody likes me? What if they think I'm weird?"

"Don't worry, little one." Her father rubbed his fin against hers. "If you want to have friends, you just have to act like a friend."

"How do I do that?" Pearl wondered.

"Always choose kindness," her father replied.

Squeak laughed and did a flip in the water. "You always say that, Daddy!" she exclaimed.

Her father smiled. "That's because it's always true."

Pearl's mother rubbed her fin against Pearl's, too. Then she gave her a gentle shove toward the entrance. "You'd better go in, Pearl," she said. "It's almost time for school to start."

2

Echo, Splash, and Flip

PEARL SWAM INTO THE SCHOOL. AT FIRST ALL she could focus on were the amazing coral formations. A tall wall of coral ringed the entire lagoon, while shorter formations divided it into smaller rooms. Tiny fish darted in and out of the spiky and spongy shapes. A pink sea anemone clung to the coral wall, its tentacles waving gracefully in the current. Nearby was a red-and-orange starfish. The reef was beautiful!

But before long, Pearl's attention shifted to the other dolphins. She'd never seen so many in one place before! Several adults were there, but most of the dolphins were Pearl's age or a little older. Youngsters came from all over this part of the Salty Sea to attend Coral Cove Dolphin School. Pearl didn't recognize a single face or voice.

Then a dolphin her age swam toward her. "Hi," she said. "I'm Echo. Are you new, too?"

"Yes. My name is Pearl," Pearl replied. She noticed that Echo had a pretty pink-striped tulip shell strung around her neck with a piece of seaweed. "I like your necklace."

"Thanks. My mom gave it to me." Echo waved over another young dolphin. "Hey, Pearl, this is Splash. He's new, too."

"Hi, Pearl!" Splash zoomed up to the surface

and leaped out. He landed with a splash and zipped back down to the girls. "I'm Splash!"

"Hi," Pearl said. "You're a good swimmer."

"Thanks." Splash sounded happy. "I can't wait until Jumping and Swimming class! What's your favorite class going to be?"

"How can we know which class will be our favorite?" Echo asked with a laugh. "We haven't started any of them yet!"

Just then, another young dolphin swam over. He was a little smaller than Pearl and the others.

"I know what *your* favorite class will be," he said, flicking his fin toward Echo. "Magic, right?"

"How do you know that?" Pearl asked him.

"Because her mom has extra strong magic," the other dolphin told her. "She once saved a whole bunch of Land Leggers from drowning."

"Is that true?" Pearl asked Echo, impressed.

"Yes." Echo sounded proud. "Their boat sank in a storm, and my mom guided them back to shore. Everyone says she was the only dolphin in the Salty Sea who could have saved them all by herself."

"I heard about that," Splash said. "Wow, your mom is famous!"

Pearl was more impressed than ever. "You must have strong magic, too, huh?" she asked Echo.

"I hope so," Echo replied. "I want to be just like my mom one day. By the way, this is Flip. He's in my pod." She wiggled a fin at the smaller dolphin.

"Hi," Splash said to Flip. "How many dolphins are in your pod?"

"Lots," Echo said. "The exact number is always changing."

"Right now there are fifty-three," Flip put in.

"Wow! Fifty-three, really?" Pearl exclaimed. "That's a lot! There are only four dolphins in my pod."

"Did you say four, or fourteen?" Splash asked in surprise.

"Four," Pearl said again. "It's just me, my mom and dad, and my little sister."

"Really? That's weird." Flip stared at Pearl.

Pearl looked at Echo and Splash. Would they think she was weird, too?

"Don't call her weird," Echo told Flip. "That's mean."

"Sorry," Flip said. But he didn't sound very sorry.

Just then, a bright blue angelfish swam past.

Splash let out an excited chirp and chased after her, circling around her and then zooming back toward Pearl and the others.

"I win!" he exclaimed with a laugh.

"That's nothing," Flip said. "Angelfish are slow. I can swim faster than a bonefish! Watch—I'll show you."

He flicked his tail, swimming halfway across the lagoon and then back again. Pearl didn't think he looked as fast as Splash. She almost said so. But then she remembered her father's words: *Always choose kindness*. Maybe it would be kinder to keep her thoughts to herself.

"How was that?" Flip asked as he reached them. "Pretty good, huh? I'll probably be the best swimmer in our class. The best jumper, too."

"Don't listen to Flip," Echo told Pearl and Splash. "He's always bragging."

"I am not!" Flip sounded insulted. "I *am* good at jumping. Watch!"

This time he zoomed up and out of the water. When he came back down, he crashed into Pearl.

"Ouch!" she cried as she bumped into a piece of sharp elkhorn coral.

"Pearl! Are you okay?" Echo swam over, sounding worried.

"You should be more careful," Splash told Flip.

"Whatever." Flip swam closer and looked at Pearl. "She didn't even get a cut."

"I'm okay," Pearl told Echo and Splash. "It's just a tiny scratch."

Echo looked relieved. Splash did a backflip

to celebrate. Pearl smiled, happy that she'd met both of them. They were exactly the kind of friends she'd hoped to make at school.

She wasn't so sure about Flip. He bragged a lot and didn't seem as nice as the others. But that was okay. There were lots of dolphins at school. Pearl was sure she could just stay out of Flip's way from now on.

3
Music Class

"ATTENTION, STUDENTS!" A VOICE RANG OUT.

Pearl turned to look toward the middle of the lagoon. Several adult dolphins were gathered there.

"Those are the teachers," Splash said, doing another backflip.

Pearl had already guessed that. But she smiled at Splash. "I hope they're nice," she said.

The largest male dolphin was the one who'd called for attention. But now he hung back as a much older male swam forward.

"Hello, all. I'm your principal," the old dolphin said. He had a deep, slow, scratchy voice that made it sound as if his insides were covered in barnacles. "You can call me Old Salty—everyone does. Now let's get started, shall we? Returning students, please go to your assigned classes. New students, come over here."

Pearl shivered with excitement. She was really here! Dolphin school was about to start!

"What class do you think we'll have first?" she asked Echo and Splash as the three of them swam toward the adults.

"I don't know, but I hope we're in the same group," Splash said. "My older brother says they'll divide us into different pods for our classes."

"Really?" Suddenly Pearl was worried.

What if she ended up in a different school pod from her new friends?

She looked around at the other new students gathering in front of the teachers. There had to be at least three dozen of them! Pearl wondered if she'd ever be able to learn all their names.

"Hello, youngsters," a female teacher said. Her voice was rich and wise. "I'm Bay. Some of you will be joining me right now for Music class. You, you, you . . ."

She waved her flipper at the students who were closest to her. Pearl was relieved when she, Echo, and Splash were all picked. Flip was in their pod, too. So were two females who kept giggling together, and two other males.

"I'm glad we're together," Echo said, rubbing her fin against Pearl's.

"Me too," Pearl said.

Bay led the class over to a quiet cove at one end of the lagoon. It was sheltered by a large reef of brain coral.

"This is the quietest area of the school," the teacher explained. "And we need peace and

quiet so we can focus on our music. As all of you know, music is a very important part of dolphin life. It's a way to communicate with others. It's a way to concentrate our magic. And of course, it's a way to create something beautiful."

She stopped talking and whistled a cheerful tune. Pearl smiled, waving her fins in time with the song. She loved music—her pod sang together all the time. A passing lionfish paused and swayed, rippling his fins in time with Bay's song.

"That was my dolphin song," Bay said when she finished. "Every dolphin has his or her own special song. It helps make each of you unique and helps you focus your magical abilities."

"Wow, cool!" Splash said.

Bay smiled. "Yes, it is cool. During this class, you will all start to develop your own special songs."

Pearl knew a little about dolphin songs. Her mother had one of the most beautiful songs Pearl could imagine. But Bay's song was amazing, too! Pearl couldn't wait to figure out her own special song.

"I already have my song worked out," Flip spoke up. "Want to hear it?"

"Yes, go ahead," Bay said.

Flip darted up to the surface to suck in some air through his blowhole. Then he came back and started to sing.

"His song isn't that good, is it?" Echo whispered to Pearl. "I think he just made it up right now. I've never heard him singing it before."

Pearl didn't say anything. She didn't want to be mean, but she agreed with Echo. Flip's song wasn't very good. It sounded the same all the way through. It wasn't nearly as beautiful and unique as Bay's song, or those of Pearl's parents.

"Very nice start," Bay said after Flip had finished. "Now, who'd like to go next? How about you, my dear?"

Pearl realized the teacher was smiling at her. "M-Me?" she stammered.

"Go ahead, Pearl," Echo urged. "Just sing what you're feeling!"

"Go, Pearl!" Splash added, flipping his fins and making bubbles swirl around him.

Pearl swam up and took a breath. She was so nervous her fins were shaking. Could she really sing in front of all these other dolphins?

Just do your best, her mother's voice said in her head.

Pearl nodded. Closing her eyes, she pretended she was in her home lagoon with Squeak. Then she began to sing. The song filled her up, making her forget everything else except the dancing notes.

When she finished, she opened her eyes. Bay's smile was wider than ever.

"Lovely!" the teacher declared. "What's your name, my dear?"

"Pearl," Pearl replied. "Was my song really okay?"

"Better than okay," Bay assured her. "You're

very talented, Pearl. I look forward to helping you finish your song. Now, who's next?"

Pearl felt amazing. She'd always loved music—but she hadn't realized she was good at it!

"Great job, Pearl!" Echo whispered as one of the other female students began to sing. "I really liked your song."

"Thanks," Pearl whispered back. "I can't wait to hear yours!"

Echo's song turned out to be pretty good. Most of the other students did fine, too. But when it was Splash's turn, he didn't do very well. His song was tuneless, and he kept getting distracted and having to start over.

"Sorry," he said at last, grinning at Bay. "I guess I'm not very good at music."

"Never mind," Bay said. "That's why we

have dolphin school—so you can all get better at the skills you need."

"But his song is terrible," Flip called out. "How can it ever get better?"

"Hey!" Echo said. "That's not nice, Flip."

Splash laughed. "It's okay. He's right. My song was terrible!"

That made everyone laugh, including Bay. "He'll get better," she told Flip. "Besides, every dolphin has different talents. I'm sure you're not good at every single thing you do, either."

"Yes, I am," Flip responded. "I'm good at everything!"

Pearl nudged Echo with her fin. "Does he always brag this much?" she whispered. "How can you stand being in the same pod with him?"

"He does brag a lot," Echo whispered back.

"But I think he's even worse today because he's nervous about starting school. He's really not so bad once you get to know him."

Pearl wasn't so sure about that. She expected Bay to scold Flip for his bragging. But the teacher just said, "Hmm," and then said it was time for Pearl's school pod to move on to Jumping and Swimming class. "Riptide will be waiting for you outside the coral," the teacher said.

4
Riptide

"HURRY UP!" RIPTIDE BELLOWED AS PEARL and the others swam out through the school entrance. "Are you dolphins, or did they send me a class of sea slugs by mistake?"

The Jumping and Swimming teacher was the large, strapping male dolphin who had called for attention earlier. He looked even bigger up close!

Just as the students reached him, Riptide turned and swam away. "Hey, wait up!" Splash exclaimed. "Where are you going?"

"No questions," Riptide said without

slowing down. "Follow me. Don't be lazy, or I'll let the sharks get you!"

Echo let out a squeak of alarm. "Come on," she said to Pearl and Splash. "We'd better keep up."

"He wouldn't really let sharks get us, would he?" Pearl wondered.

Flip heard her and laughed. "Why, are you scared?" he asked. "I'm not. I can outswim any stupid old shark in the sea!"

Pearl ignored him. She was too busy trying to keep up with Riptide and the others. She never had to swim that fast at home!

Riptide led them away from the reef. He stopped in an area of open water. Pearl looked around, her eyes wide and nervous.

"Is this Bigsky Basin?" she asked.

Riptide barked out a laugh. "Don't be

silly!" he said. "Bigsky Basin is much deeper than this. I brought you out here so we'll have space to move around. This is Jumping and Swimming class, and that's exactly what you'll be doing. Jumping and swimming!"

"Yay!" Splash cheered, doing a flip.

Riptide laughed again. "You, young fellow," he said. "I bet you can do a flip in the air, eh?"

"Sure! Want to see?" Splash said. He shot up toward the surface and did a high flip, landing with a big *splash*!

"Excellent!" Riptide roared out. "Now, who's next?"

"Me!" Flip volunteered. "My name is Flip, and that means I'm the best at doing flips. Just watch!"

Pearl had to admit that Flip's flip was very good. After that, the two giggling female

students took their turns. Both of their flips were good as well.

"Excellent!" Riptide sounded pleased. "It looks like I've got a good class here. Now, who's next?"

Pearl hung back as long as she could. She'd never even tried to do an air flip before! But finally it was her turn. She zoomed up toward the surface and burst out into the air. The sun was bright, and it was hard to see up there. She did her best to do a flip like the others, but she landed on her side and sank down.

"Oof!" Flip called out with a laugh. "Hey, Pearl, you're supposed to do a flip, not a flop!"

Riptide blew out a stream of bubbles. "All right, it seems some of us have some work to do," he said. "Next?"

Pearl floated back over to her friends. "Never mind," Echo said, rubbing Pearl's fin with her own. "Like Bay said, not everyone is good at everything, right?"

That made Pearl feel a little better. At least for a moment.

But after that, the class just kept getting harder. All the other dolphins seemed to be stronger and faster than she was. She kept having trouble with jumping and couldn't keep up with the others while swimming. By the end of class, Pearl was exhausted.

"I never have to do any of this stuff at home!" she told her friends, sinking nearly to the seafloor.

"It's okay," Echo said. "You'll get better if you work at it."

"Yeah," Splash agreed. "I'll help you if you want. And maybe you can help me with music, since you're so good at that."

"It's a deal!" Pearl said.

Just then Flip swam over. "That was fun," he said. "Well, for me at least." He smirked at Pearl, then swam off.

"What a shark face!" Echo whispered as Flip started bragging to the rest of the pod.

"Yeah." But Flip's comment didn't bother Pearl. At least not very much. Not when Echo and Splash were already feeling like such good friends.

5
Mullet's Tour

WHEN PEARL AND THE OTHERS SWAM BACK into the school lagoon, Bay was waiting for them. "Time for recess, young ones," she said. "All the students have a break now. Go play and get to know the rest of your classmates!"

Pearl looked around. All the other new students were already out in the middle of the lagoon. So were the older students. Some dolphins were playing tag or having a snack. Others were just talking.

"Look, there's Finny." Splash waved a fin at

one of the older dolphins. "That's my brother. Let's go say hi!"

Pearl followed him. So did Echo. Flip tagged along, too. "*My* brother already graduated," Flip said. "He was the best jumper in the whole school. But everyone says I'm even better!"

"That's nice," Pearl said. She wished Flip would stop bragging.

Splash's brother was blowing bubbles with two other dolphins his age.

"Hey, Splash," he said. "Meet Mullet and Shelly. They're in my school pod."

"Hi," Mullet said to them in a friendly voice. "Welcome to Coral Cove Dolphin School."

"Yeah, hi," Shelly added. She whistled a little tune. "That's my welcome song. Do you like it?"

"It's pretty," Pearl said, impressed. Shelly seemed really talented!

"We already had Music class," Flip told the older students. "I was probably the best one there. The others did okay, too, though. I guess."

"You shouldn't brag so much," Echo told him.

"It's not bragging when it's true," Flip replied, doing a flip in the water.

"Nice flip," Mullet told him. "You must be good at Jumping and Swimming class, too, huh?"

"Definitely!" Flip did another flip. "I'm great at all that stuff."

Just then, Bay swam over to the group. "I'll be right back, youngsters," she said. "Old Salty asked me to help him shoo away some jellyfish that are floating in his class area."

"Ooh, I'll come help," Shelly said. "I've been working on my magical guiding skills. I'd love to try them out on some jellyfish!"

"I'll come, too," Finny said.

"While they're doing that, why don't I give the new kids a tour of the rest of the lagoon?" Mullet suggested. "Is that all right, Bay?"

"Hmm." Bay flicked her flukes. "I suppose so. Make sure you're back in time for their next class, though. Old Salty doesn't like his students to be late."

"I promise," Mullet said. "Come on, let's go!"

Pearl, Echo, Splash, and Flip followed Mullet as he swam out through the coral entrance. "A tour sounds fun," Echo said. "What are you going to show us out here?"

"That's for me to know and you to find out," Mullet said.

Pearl was surprised. Mullet didn't sound as friendly and nice as he had a few minutes earlier.

"We probably shouldn't swim too far away," Pearl said. "I don't want to be late for class."

Mullet ignored her. "Let's see you flip again," he told Flip. "But stay totally underwater this time if you can."

"Sure, I can do that!" Flip said eagerly. He started an underwater flip.

He was halfway around when his movements suddenly got faster. He spun around and around.

Mullet laughed. "Hey!" Echo said to him. "Are you doing that?"

Pearl wasn't that close to Mullet, but she could feel magic energy coming from him. He was pushing Flip with his magic, just like Pearl's mother had done with the eel earlier.

"Help!" Flip cried. "I can't stop!"

Mullet laughed again. "Say, 'Mullet is great,' and maybe you will," he said.

"Mullet is great! Mullet is great!" Flip cried.

Finally he stopped spinning. He sank toward the seafloor, looking dizzy.

"You used magical guiding on him—no, I bet it was magical pushing!" Echo accused Mullet. "You're not supposed to use that on other dolphins!"

"Not unless there's an emergency," Splash added.

Mullet smirked. "This *was* an emergency," he said. "You guys are so boring I thought I might die."

"I'm telling the teachers what you just did." Echo sounded angry.

"You'd better not!" Mullet stopped laughing and glared at her. "Or else!"

"Or else what?" Echo demanded.

Pearl shivered. Now Mullet looked really

mean! She was impressed that Echo was being so brave.

"Or else I might shove you out into Bigsky Basin with the sharks!" Mullet said.

Pearl let out a squeak of alarm—Echo had started moving backward through the water toward Bigsky Basin!

"Hey!" Echo yelled. "Stop that, or I'll send a mental message to the teachers! My mom taught me how!"

Echo stopped moving.

"Relax, I was just kidding around," Mullet said with a laugh. "I'm trying to show you all the cool stuff you'll learn in Magic class. I didn't think you'd get so upset."

"*I'm* not upset," Flip said. "You're really good at magic, Mullet. I'll probably be just as good when I'm your age."

"See?" Mullet told Echo. "Flip isn't mad, so I hope you're not, either. It was just for fun. No hard feelings?"

Echo looked uncertain. Finally she flicked her flukes.

"I guess it's okay," she said. "We should go back, though."

Pearl was relieved when the whole group swam toward the school entrance. Mullet's tour hadn't been much fun. But at least nothing really bad had happened.

6
Dolphin Magic

HALFWAY THROUGH OCEAN LORE CLASS, Pearl felt sleepy. Old Salty was teaching them about animals and plants in the ocean. Right then he was listing different types of mollusks. Before that, he'd listed different types of sea sponges. And before that, he'd listed different types of algae. After a while, all the names sounded the same.

"How does he expect us to remember all this stuff?" Splash whispered to Pearl.

"I don't know," Pearl whispered back.

She was glad that Magic class came next.

That was sure to be more interesting than learning about algae!

Finally Old Salty stopped talking. "I'm sorry to say that's all we have time for today, young scholars," he said in his crusty voice. "Tomorrow we'll discuss crustaceans. Off to Magic class with you now—Bay is waiting for you over by the kelp forest."

Pearl swam with her friends toward the waving strands of kelp at the far end of the cove. She could hear the other two girls from their class complaining about how boring Old Salty was.

"I already forgot everything he said," one of them exclaimed.

"I never heard it in the first place," her friend said. "I was taking a nap."

"I remember everything," Flip bragged.

"I have an awesome memory."

Pearl rolled her eyes.

They reached Bay at the kelp forest. "Welcome to Magic class, everyone," she said. Suddenly Pearl and her classmates were surrounded by sparkly lights and colorful swirls of water. Pearl had seen displays like that before. Her mother was especially good at them. She used her magic to make them out of sunlight and water droplets. Dolphins sometimes used the magical displays to distract other creatures, but mostly they were just for fun.

"Cool!" one of the other students exclaimed. "Will we learn to do that?"

"Yes, but not right away," Bay said as the display faded. "We'll learn the basics of all the most important kinds of dolphin magic in this class. That includes guiding and messaging, the two most important types of mental magic. Most of you are probably at least a little bit familiar with those."

Pearl nodded along with the others. She had liked Bay during Music class, and she was glad that Bay was their Magic teacher, too.

"What about mental confusion?" Splash asked. "Will we learn that, too? A dolphin in my pod used that once to escape from a hungry orca."

"That's very advanced mental magic," Echo told him.

Bay nodded. "Echo is right. It's a powerful tool against bigger creatures, but you won't learn that until next year. This year, though, in addition to mental magic, we'll also begin to study physical magic. For instance, you'll learn how to make sounds louder or softer, and to create light and rainbows. We'll also begin to develop your magical healing abilities."

"Awesome," Pearl said. She couldn't wait!

"Let's start today with magical guiding," Bay said. "Does anyone already know how to do that?"

"I do," Echo said, flicking her fins. "At least a little bit. My mom taught me."

"Why don't you show the class?" Bay said. "See if you can guide that sea horse over there to turn around and swim the other way."

"I'll try." Echo swam closer to a little orange sea horse swimming nearby.

Pearl could tell that her friend was focusing hard. She could feel magical energy coming from Echo.

The sea horse slowed down. Then he stopped—and turned to swim in the opposite direction!

"Excellent!" Bay exclaimed. "Your mother taught you well."

"Let me try," Flip said. "I bet I can do that, too."

"All right, give it a try," Bay told him.

Flip swam over to the sea horse. He closed his eyes and started sending out bursts of magical energy. This time, the sea horse didn't turn around. After a few minutes Flip gave up.

"I probably didn't have enough air left,"

he said, darting up to the surface and then returning. "Besides, this stuff is boring. When will we learn how to make one of those light displays?"

"We'll get to that on another day," Bay said. "Now, would anyone else like to see if they can guide the sea horse?"

Pearl wiggled her fin uncertainly. "I don't know how to use real magical guiding yet," she said. "But I can try asking the sea horse to turn by sending him a mental message."

"Oh?" Bay looked impressed. "You have experience with sending messages to other species?"

Pearl nodded. "My family helps baby turtles find their way out to sea," she explained. "I practice sending the turtles messages sometimes."

"Wonderful." Bay waved a fin at the sea horse. "Go ahead and give it a try."

Pearl swam closer to the sea horse. He was floating in one spot now, watching her.

Closing her eyes, Pearl formed a picture in her mind of the sea horse swimming away. She gathered her magical energy and sent the image out toward the creature.

Then she opened her eyes. Had it worked?

Yes! The sea horse was swimming away, just as Pearl had pictured!

"Great job, Pearl!" Echo cheered. Splash did a happy flip to celebrate.

Bay seemed impressed, too. "Helping sea turtles is important work," she told Pearl. "I'd be interested in hearing more about your pod later."

"Sure," Pearl said shyly.

"All right, class," Bay said. "The rest of us will learn to send messages to other species later. We'll also learn more about guiding on another day. Now, let's focus on messaging other dolphins. As you know, that's how we can communicate with one another at long distances . . ."

She went on to explain how to focus their energy to send messages. Once again, Echo went first when it was time to try. This time Pearl helped by swimming to the other side of the kelp forest. A moment later, she received Echo's message: *Swim back here now.*

Echo turned out to be the best at messaging, though Pearl did fine, too, thanks to all her practice with Squeak. Splash wasn't very good at it, though. He couldn't get his message out at all until Pearl touched his fin to join her magical energy with his. Suddenly, Splash's message (which was *I love jumping!*) beamed out to the whole class!

"Very nice," Bay told Splash and Pearl with a smile. "Our magic is always strongest when we work together."

Almost before Pearl knew it, class was over. "We'll continue working on messaging tomorrow, along with some basic guiding," Bay said. "We'll also start learning about how to use music to make our magic stronger."

Pearl wished tomorrow would hurry up and arrive. She couldn't wait to learn all that stuff. Magic was fun!

7

Mullet's Scary Dare

"WHAT DID YOU THINK OF YOUR FIRST DAY OF school?" Echo asked Pearl and Splash as the three of them swam out of the lagoon.

"It was super!" Splash did a flip.

"How can you say that?" Flip asked, swimming over to join them. "You were terrible at Music, Splash. You weren't that great at Magic, either."

"I know." Splash laughed. "But that's why we go to school, right? To get better at that stuff."

"In that case, I shouldn't bother to come

back tomorrow," Flip said. "I'm already the best at everything!"

Pearl didn't think that was true. But once again, she remembered what her father had said to her that morning: *Always choose kindness.*

It wouldn't be kind to tell Flip he wasn't as good as he thought he was, Pearl decided. So she kept quiet.

Just then Mullet swam up to them. "Are you still bragging about how great you are?" he asked Flip. "If you're so great, I think you should prove it."

"Okay, watch this." Flip did a double flip. "Pretty awesome, huh?"

"That's nothing. Anyone can do a silly flip." Mullet did one himself. "If you really want to prove you're great, you should swim across Bigsky Basin."

"Why would I do that?" Flip said. "Anyone can swim in open water. But not everyone can flip like me!"

"Besides, Bigsky Basin isn't safe," Echo put in. "There might be sharks out there."

"Exactly," Mullet smirked. "If Flip is the best swimmer, he'll have no trouble outswimming a shark or two."

"That's true," Flip said. "Sharks don't scare me!"

"Prove it," Mullet said. "I dare you!"

"Don't listen to him, Flip," Echo said. "Come on, we should go find our pod."

Mullet ignored them. "Are you scared, Flip?" he taunted. "I thought you were the best swimmer."

"I am." Flip blew a burst of bubbles out of his blowhole. "And I'll do it! Just watch me."

"Come on," Mullet said. "I'll swim with you to the edge of the Basin right now."

"You can't!" Pearl blurted out in shock. She didn't trust Mullet.

"Don't do it, Flip!" Echo added.

"You can't tell me what to do," Flip said. "I'm not scared."

"You should be," Splash said. "Sharks are scary! My pod ran into this huge bull shark once. We had to swim super fast to get away!"

Flip flicked his flukes. "Sharks are only scary for spineless jellyfish, like you guys," he said. "I'm going, and that's that!"

8

A Mysterious Message

Flip swam away with Mullet. Pearl watched him go, feeling worried.

"What if Mullet puts Flip in danger?" she said. "Should we tell the teachers where they're going?"

Echo blew out a small stream of bubbles. "I don't know. Flip isn't as brave as he acts, though, so as soon as they get to the Basin, he'll probably swim away and hide like a hermit crab in its shell."

Pearl hoped she was right. "I guess we should swim home. I want to tell my pod all about today."

"We'll swim part of the way with you if you want," Splash offered.

Pearl smiled at him. "Thanks. That would be great."

She, Splash, and Echo set out through the warm, shallow waters near the school. Fish were everywhere. A stingray swam past, and a few minutes later the dolphins were surrounded by a huge school of sleek, silvery mackerel.

After the little silver fish passed, Pearl could see the sun shining down into deeper water off to the left. Echo saw her looking that way.

"That's Bigsky Basin over there," Echo said. "Don't worry, it's just the edge."

"I know." Pearl shivered, imagining how many sharks might be out there.

"So what was your favorite class today, Pearl?" Splash asked, distracting Pearl from her scary thoughts.

"Magic, definitely," Pearl said. "Music class was great, too."

"You're really good at music," Splash told her. "And Echo, you're amazing at magic!"

"Only because my mom taught me." Echo blew out a curtain of bubbles to hide her face. "You guys will be just as good as me soon."

"Maybe," Pearl said. She sighed. "But I'll never be any good at jumping and swimming."

"Sure you will." Splash nudged her with his fin. "You just need to practice."

"Riptide is a little scary, though, isn't he?" Echo said.

Pearl nodded, relieved that she wasn't the only one who thought that. "Definitely!" she said.

"He's not that bad. He's just trying to make us the best we can be," Splash said, doing a quick flip in the water. "All the teachers are. They want us to learn a lot so we'll be just as good at everything as they are."

Pearl knew he was probably right. But it was hard to imagine ever being that good at everything.

"I have to turn here to get to my lagoon," she said as they passed a craggy coral formation swarming with colorful fish. "I can go on alone from here."

"Are you sure?" Splash said. "Then I'll guess we'll see you tomorrow."

"Yep!" Pearl was already looking forward

to her second day of school. "See you tomorr—"

She cut herself off with a burst of bubbles. She'd just received a sudden strong mental message!

"What's wrong?" Splash asked her.

"A message," Pearl blurted out. Her mind was filled with pictures, but they were changing so fast she couldn't make them out. "I'm getting it right now. A really strong one!"

"A message?" Splash sounded confused. "Who is it from?"

Echo closed her eyes. "I feel it, too," she said. "It's really cloudy, though." She sounded frustrated. "I wish my mom were here! She'd be able to get the message with no trouble at all."

"What can you see, Pearl?" Splash asked.

"I—I'm not sure." Pearl swam up and pulled in some air through her blowhole. Then she sank back down toward her friends, focusing on the images filling her mind.

At first she thought the message might be coming from one of the sea creatures nearby— maybe that horseshoe crab swimming past, or one of the oysters on the seafloor below. But even though it was only pictures instead of words, somehow she was sure it was coming from a dolphin.

That was strange. Because until today's Magic class, Pearl had never received a mental message from another dolphin except for Squeak and her parents. Usually she only got messages from turtles or some of the other creatures in her lagoon. But this message was much stronger than those ever were.

"What do you see?" Splash asked. "Maybe we can help you figure it out."

Pearl focused even harder. "I see water with lots of sunlight coming through," she said. "Wait! I'm finally getting words, too!"

She focused even harder, trying to hear the message: *Help! Help me! Please help me!*

Echo gasped. Pearl could tell she was

working hard at her magic. "I think it's coming from Flip!" Echo cried.

Pearl blew out all her air in a rush as another picture jumped into her mind. "Oh no!" she cried. "It's a shark!"

9
To the Rescue

"A SHARK? WHERE?" SPLASH CRIED, SPINNING around.

"Not here," Pearl told him. "I saw it in Flip's message. He seems scared. He must have run into a shark in Bigsky Basin!"

"This is terrible!" Echo exclaimed. "We have to get help!"

Flip's terrified words rushed through Pearl's mind again: *Help! Help me! Please help me!*

Pearl looked back the way they'd come. "We could swim back to school," she said. "The teachers are probably still there. They all have much stronger magic than we do—they could save Flip from that shark for sure."

"Sure they could." Echo sounded anxious. "But can we get to them in time? Even you might not be fast enough, Splash."

"Maybe we can try sending the adults a mental message," Splash suggested. "You two are both good at that magic stuff."

"But I've only practiced at short distances!" By now Echo sounded frantic. "And Pearl is only used to sending messages to turtles!"

Another cry for help came into Pearl's mind. "It sounds like the shark is really close," she said. "There's no time to get the adults. We have to help Flip ourselves!"

"Us?" Echo said. "But what can we do? We're just kids!"

Splash looked uncertain and scared, but he

nodded. "Pearl is right. Aren't we the defenders of the ocean? Let's go defend Flip from that shark!"

"O-Okay." Echo sounded nervous. "But how?"

Pearl started swimming in the direction of the deeper water. "I don't know," she said. "Let's try sending mental messages to the adults while we're swimming. Maybe one of them is closer than we think."

She felt a little better after having that idea. Focusing her magical energy, she sent out a message asking for help. She could feel her friends doing the same thing.

"I'm not sure mine is working," Splash said, reaching for his friends' fins. "Let's join our energy. That should make it work better."

They sent out their message again. By then

they were entering deeper water. The seafloor fell away quickly, and soon Pearl could barely see it through the murky darkness. The sun's cheerful light didn't reach far into the deeper parts of the Salty Sea.

"How are we going to find Flip?" Splash asked. "Bigsky Basin is huge!"

Pearl turned until she felt the message getting stronger. "This way, I think."

The others followed her. "I think I see something up ahead," Echo said after a moment.

Pearl swam faster. Soon she spotted Flip floating in the water just below the surface. Circling him was an enormous tiger shark! Mullet was nowhere in sight.

"Oh no!" Echo whispered. "That thing is huge!"

Splash looked nervous, too. "What can we do to help Flip?" he whispered. "That shark is big enough to swallow all four of us in one gulp!"

"Maybe we could find some seaweed and try to tangle him up in it," Echo said. "I heard sharks can't breathe if they stop swimming."

"That won't work." Splash did a backflip.

"For one thing, it would take too long to find enough seaweed."

"Okay, maybe we should all crash into the shark at once," Echo said. "We could hit him with our flukes, too. That might confuse him."

Splash looked dubious. "That sounds pretty dangerous. We need a better plan than that!"

Pearl tried to come up with a better plan. Her friends were making it hard to think, though. Echo was blowing air out of her blowhole in short bursts, creating a sea of bubbles. And Splash was so nervous he kept doing flips.

Watching her friends suddenly gave Pearl an idea. The dolphins weren't strong enough to fight the shark, or fast enough to outswim it. But they did have their own special skills.

"We need to distract the shark, right?" she said. "That might give Flip enough time to get away. Maybe we can do that by working together."

She quickly explained her plan. Her friends nodded.

"That just might work," Echo said hopefully.

"Let's do it," Splash agreed.

Pearl floated to the surface and took a deep breath. Then she started singing, whistling a lively tune. She tried to remember the song she'd heard her father use once to soothe an angry squid. Pearl's song didn't sound exactly like that, but it was pretty close.

At the same time, Echo started sending out magical energy. She used it to make Pearl's music louder. They hadn't worked on that sort of magic in class yet, but Echo knew how to do it thanks to her mother's lessons.

The shark moved a little farther away from Flip. He seemed to be looking at the other dolphins now, though Pearl couldn't tell for sure. He floated closer, moving slowly, his tail flicking in time to Pearl's song.

"It's working!" Echo told Pearl. "We're distracting the shark."

"But now he's coming right at us!" Pearl was so nervous that she forgot to keep singing. The shark kept swimming toward them.

Echo sent out a big burst of bubbles that floated off to the left. The shark slowed, looking that way.

"Hey, shark breath!" Splash shouted. While the girls were distracting the shark, he'd swum off to one side to do his part. "Over here, dorsal face!"

He started doing flips and spins, churning up the water. The shark turned again, moving toward Splash this time.

"Quick, start singing!" Echo cried to Pearl. "Otherwise he's going to catch Splash!"

The shark was swimming faster now, aiming straight at Splash. His mouth opened wide, showing his jagged teeth. Splash let out a squeak and darted to one side, but the shark followed his movement.

"Sing, Pearl, sing!" Echo cried.

Pearl started singing again. She made the song as loud as she could, but she wasn't sure the shark could hear it.

Then Echo sent out a burst of magic energy. The song got louder, and the shark slowed. This time when Splash darted to one side, the shark didn't follow. He turned back around and stared at the girls.

Pearl kept singing. At the same time, she noticed that Flip was still floating in the water nearby. He didn't look hurt, so Pearl guessed that he was too scared to move.

Go! she told him in a mental message. *Get out of here!*

She wasn't sure the message had worked. But finally Flip started moving. He swam off in the opposite direction. A moment later he'd disappeared in the gloomy water.

"Good, he's safe." Echo had seen Flip swim away, too. "Now how are we going to get out of here?"

Before Pearl could answer, the shark burst into motion again. He spun around and shot toward Splash, who had stopped swimming while the shark was distracted.

"Splash, look out!" Echo cried, magical energy exploding out of her in all directions.

"The song isn't working anymore!" Pearl exclaimed. "We have to do something!"

10

A Close Call

PEARL'S HEART POUNDED. SPLASH WAS swimming as fast as he could. But the big shark was faster! The only way Splash could stay ahead of the shark's deadly jaws was by twisting and turning in circles. The shark was so big that he couldn't turn as fast.

"Splash can't keep that up for long," Echo said, her voice shaking.

"I know. And if he swims in a straight line, the shark will catch him." Pearl had never been so scared in her life. "What are we going to do?"

"We could try to confuse the shark's mind," Echo said. "Magically, I mean."

"But that's really advanced magic—you said so yourself!" Pearl said. "We won't even start studying it until next year."

She felt ready to give up. Her plan had gone wrong, and now the shark was going to eat Splash!

But Echo looked determined and brave. "Mom taught me a little," she said. "Anyway, we have to try something!" Echo reached for Pearl's fin. "Come on, Pearl. Just add your magic to mine . . ."

Pearl could feel Echo trying to send a strange, confusing whirl of magical energy toward the shark. Would it work? Pearl knew that mental confusion had saved her father from the shark that had left that scar on his dorsal fin. It had happened when he was just a little older than Pearl was now. His pod had confused the creature's mind just long enough for him to get away.

For a moment it seemed to be working on this shark, too. He slowed down again, turning halfway toward the girls. Pearl felt a surge of hope.

But after a second, the shark shook his whole body and then turned back toward Splash. "Our magic isn't strong enough!" Echo cried. "It's not working!"

Suddenly a sleek gray shape appeared out of the darkness. Pearl spun around, afraid that all the commotion might have attracted another shark. But it wasn't a shark at all.

"Flip!" she cried.

"Here, let me help." Flip touched his fin to Pearl's, then wrapped his tail around Echo's. Magical energy started pouring out of him.

Pearl gasped. "Echo, keep trying to confuse him! Maybe it will work with all three of us helping!"

And it did! The shark slowed down, and finally stopped chasing Splash altogether. He floated in the water, turning in slow circles. His black eyes looked dull and unfocused.

"Swim, Splash!" Echo cried. "Hurry! We'll follow you!"

Splash darted away from the shark, heading for the edge of Bigsky Basin. Pearl, Echo, and Flip followed. But they didn't stop sending the confusing energy until the shark faded out of sight behind them.

By the time they reached the shallows near the reefs, Pearl was exhausted. "Wow, magic is hard," she said, blowing out a few tired bubbles.

Splash floated to the surface for a breath, then returned to the others. "Thanks for saving me, you guys," he said. "I thought I was about to become that shark's dinner!"

"M-Me too." Flip hadn't said anything since they'd left the shark behind. "Thanks for coming to save me."

"You're welcome," Pearl told him. "Thanks for coming back to help us save Splash."

Just then there was a loud whistle up ahead. A moment later, Riptide and Bay burst into view, swimming toward the kids with a rush of bubbles pouring out behind them. "Are you all right?" Riptide exclaimed. "We came as soon as we got your message!"

"Yes," Bay said. "Nice work with the message, by the way. But what happened?"

Flip swam forward. "I'll tell you all about it," he said.

Pearl looked over at Echo. Was Flip about to start bragging again? Would he tell the teachers he'd saved all of them, instead of the other way around? That seemed like something he would do.

But he didn't. Instead he told the teachers exactly what had happened. "I'm sorry I accepted that dare," he said after he finished his story. "It was stupid to swim out into Bigsky Basin all alone."

"You say young Mullet dared you to do it?" Riptide sounded surprised. "That doesn't sound like him. He's a fine student—very athletic, kind to everyone, never puts a fin wrong. You probably misunderstood him."

Pearl and Echo traded another look. Riptide's

description didn't sound like Mullet at all!

"Hmm," Bay said. "Well, it seems everyone is safe now. Would you like us to swim you home?"

"That's all right," Echo said. "We can all swim Pearl home first, since her pod lives the farthest away. Then Flip and I can drop off Splash with his pod on our way back to our own." She looked at Flip. "Right?"

"Sure," Flip said. "It'll be fun."

And it was! Pearl was surprised by how smart and funny Flip could be when he wasn't bragging. Maybe she hadn't only made two new friends on her first day of school. Maybe she'd made three!

What an exciting day it had been. She couldn't wait to see what new adventures her second day at Coral Cove Dolphin School would bring!

Read on for a sneak

peek at the next

story!

Echo's
Lucky Charm

"WHAT DO YOU MEAN, YOUR SHELL IS GONE?"
Pearl swam closer to her. Sure enough, there
was no sign of Echo's necklace! It was strange
to see her not wearing it.

"Oh no!" Echo cried again, spinning around
in the water. "The seaweed string must have
broken during class."

"Probably," Flip agreed. "You hit the water
pretty hard a few times doing all that tail
walking."

"I have to go back and find it!" Echo
exclaimed.

"You can't," Splash said. "Ocean Lore starts
in a few minutes. You'll get in trouble if you're
late."

"I don't care." Echo sounded frantic. "I have to find my shell!"

Pearl was worried, too. Echo's lucky shell was really special. But she also didn't want her friend to get in trouble for skipping class.

"We'll help you find it right after school," she said. "We promise. Right, guys?"

"Right!" Splash said, and Flip nodded.

Echo hesitated, still staring out through the entrance toward the open water outside. But finally she nodded, too.

"Okay," she said. "I guess I can wait."

Ocean Lore seemed to pass even more slowly than usual. Old Salty spent the first half of the class talking about the feeding habits of tube worms. Then he switched to describing the different types of sea slugs in the area. Pearl was pretty sure she wouldn't remember anything the teacher was saying. She was too worried about Echo. What if they couldn't find her lucky shell?

Finally, Old Salty dismissed them. Magic class was next. As Pearl and her friends swam past the school entrance, Echo paused.

"I wish I could go look for my shell now instead of waiting," she said. "What if the current carries it away?"

"The current isn't very strong where we were," Splash pointed out.

Pearl touched Echo's fin. "Come on. We only have one more class, and then we'll find your shell."

Echo nodded and followed Pearl and the boys. But as soon as they reached the Magic area, she swam over to Bay.

"May I be excused for a few minutes?"

Echo asked the teacher. "I lost my lucky shell during Jumping and Swimming, and I need to go out and find it."

"I'm sorry, Echo," Bay said. "You'll have to do that after class. The test is the day after tomorrow, and we have a lot to work to do before then."

"But I won't do as well without my lucky magic shell," Echo argued. "I won't be gone long."

"I said no, Echo." Bay's voice was kind but firm. "Now take your spot and let's get started."

Echo stared at the teacher for a moment without moving or saying anything. Finally she turned with a flip of her tail and swam over to Pearl.

"Can you believe she's being so mean?"

Echo whispered. "I thought she'd understand!"

Pearl gave her a sympathetic look. But she didn't say anything, since Bay was already talking about the lesson plan for that day.

"We'll start by reviewing what we did yesterday," the teacher was saying. "Since some of you had trouble guiding the school of fish, we're going to back up to a smaller number of creatures." She waved a fin at three cute little striped coral shrimp clinging to a piece of mushroom coral on the sea floor. "I'd like each of you to guide those shrimp to climb down off the coral. Now, who wants to go first?"

Pearl expected Echo to volunteer, like she usually did. But Echo was staring at the sea floor, looking distracted and anxious.

"I'll try!" Flip called out. "I'll probably do

great without Splash holding me back." He glanced at Splash. "No offense."

Flip swam up for a breath of air. Then he returned and focused on the shrimp. It took him a long time, but he finally got two of them to hop down from the coral. The third one stayed where she was, but Bay still looked pleased.

"Well done, Flip," she said. "Who else would like to give it a try? Echo, how about you?"

"I guess," Echo muttered. While Bay guided the shrimp back onto the coral, Echo swam slowly up to the surface to take a breath and sank even more slowly back down.

"What's taking her so long?" Pearl heard Harmony whisper just behind her.

"Go ahead," Bay said. "Whenever you're ready, Echo."

Echo sent out a burst of magic energy. One of the shrimp moved a few steps toward the edge of the coral. But the other two stayed still.

Pearl held her breath, expecting Echo to try again. Instead, she felt the magic energy stop. Echo backed away and looked at Bay.

"I can't do it," she said. "Not without my lucky shell."

"Nonsense," Bay said firmly. "Try again, please."

Echo frowned, looking as if she wanted to argue. Instead, she swam back over to the shrimp and sent out another weak burst of energy.

"Go, Echo!" Splash cheered. "You can do it!"

But the shrimp didn't budge. They just sat there, their long antennae waving in the current.

"Come on, Echo," Bay said. "I know you can do better than that."

"No, I can't!" Echo sent out a sudden wild burst of magic energy. The shrimp all jumped up as if an electric ray had just shocked them, then leaped off the coral. One scuttled off across the sea floor, while the others hid under the coral's wavy edge.

Bay frowned. "I asked you to guide them, not push them."

Pearl's eyes widened in surprise. Pushing was related to guiding, but more advanced— and much less nice. While guiding was a way of asking creatures to do something, pushing was a way of forcing them. Dolphins weren't supposed to push other creatures unless it was absolutely necessary.

"I didn't mean to!" Echo's muzzle quivered,

and her fins flapped in distress. "It's hard to control my magic without my shell to help."

Bay didn't say anything for a moment. Finally, she blew out a narrow stream of bubbles.

"All right, let me gather the shrimp again," she said. "Harmony, you can go next."

Pearl reached for Echo's fin when she swam back over. But Echo kept her fins close to her body, out of reach.

Pearl wasn't sure what to think about how her friend was acting. She was used to Echo being the most talented in the class at magic. Could it really just have been her lucky shell all along?

The Rescue Princesses

These are no ordinary princesses—
they're Rescue Princesses!

Puppy Powers

Get your paws on the Puppy Powers series!

There's something special about the animals at Power's Pets . . . something downright magical!

Secret Kingdom

Be in on the secret.
Collect them all!

Enjoy six sparkling adventures.

RAINBOW magic™

Which Magical Fairies Have You Met?

- ❏ The Rainbow Fairies
- ❏ The Weather Fairies
- ❏ The Jewel Fairies
- ❏ The Pet Fairies
- ❏ The Dance Fairies
- ❏ The Music Fairies
- ❏ The Sports Fairies
- ❏ The Party Fairies
- ❏ The Ocean Fairies
- ❏ The Night Fairies
- ❏ The Magical Animal Fairies
- ❏ The Princess Fairies
- ❏ The Superstar Fairies
- ❏ The Fashion Fairies
- ❏ The Sugar & Spice Fairies
- ❏ The Earth Fairies
- ❏ The Magical Crafts Fairies

📖 SCHOLASTIC

Find all of your favorite fairy friends at
scholastic.com/rainbowmagic

RMFAIRY11